MEXICO

W9-CGU-066

Palaces and temples
Canals
Causeways

How to pronounce some of the difficult words in this book:

Calhuacan	*Cal-wah-can*
calmecac	*kal-me-kak*
Ciuacoatl	*See-wah-co-atl*
Cortés	*Cor-tezz*
Huitzilopochtli	*Wee-tzeel-o-potch-tly*
Ixtacihuatl	*Ees-ta-kee-wah-tl*
maquihuitl	*ma-ki-weetl*
mayeques	*my-e-kwez*
Moctezuma Xocoyotzin	*Mok-tay-zoo-ma Sho-coy-ot-seen*
Panfilo de Narváez	*Pan-fee-lo day Nar-vay-es*
Popocatapetl	*Popo-kat-ay-petl*
Quetzalcoatl	*Kayt-zal-co-atl*
tamales	*tam-ah-lez*
Tenochtitlan	*Ten-otch-ti-tlan*
Texcoco	*Tesh-ko-ko*
tortillas	*tor-tee-yas*
Yacatecuhtli	*Yak-a-tay-coot-ly*

Acknowledgments: The photograph of the Aztec mask on the title page is reproduced by permission of the British Museum, and the photograph of the Aztec feathered head-dress on page 46 by permission of the Museum für Volkerkunde, Vienna. Photographs on pages 22, 23, 24-25, 45, 51, and title page are by Robert Harding Associates, on page 19 by Popperfoto, and on page 42 by Tourist Photo Library.

Published by Ladybird Books Ltd Loughborough Leicestershire UK
Ladybird Books Inc Lewiston Maine 04240 USA

Great Civilisations
The Aztecs

by BRENDA RALPH LEWIS
with illustrations by ROBERT AYTON

Ladybird Books

The flint blade of the sacrificial knife flashed in the sunshine as the Aztec priest raised it high in the air. Directly below, a man lay face upwards across a stone altar, held down by his arms and legs by four more priests. Death was only moments away now. The knife plunged down, piercing deep into the man's chest. Seconds later, the heart had been torn out and with a cry of triumph, the priest who had performed the sacrifice was holding it up towards the Sun.

The five priests and their victim were alone on top of a great stepped pyramid 90 ft (27.5 m) high. All the same, the sacrifice had been witnessed by a great crowd of people. They milled about far below in the *tecpan* (temple enclosure) of Tenochtitlan, the capital city the Aztecs had built on Lake Texcoco, in central Mexico.

When they saw that the sacrifice had been performed, the crowd gave a great sigh of satisfaction. For the great Sun god, Huitzilopochtli, had been supplied with another offering of human heart and blood. And before the sun went down that evening Huitzilopochtli would have an even greater store of this precious life-giving material. For at the base of the pyramid, another victim waited. Behind him, standing in line, were more victims. Throughout the afternoon, they climbed one by one up the steps of the pyramid. By the time the sky began to darken, all had been sacrificed.

The crowd of watchers began to disperse. Very soon, night would fall. Even though the streets and canals of Tenochtitlan were well lit with burning braziers, the Aztecs dreaded the hours of darkness.

Then, they believed, demons and ghosts were every-where. Besides, Tenochtitlan was 7,400 ft (2,255 m) above sea level, and that high up in mountain country, it grew intensely cold very soon after sunset. The Aztecs were only lightly clad, in loincloths, and their feet were bare. Those who had cloaks huddled into them as they hurried away along the mud paths that led towards the canals. There, they had moored their canoes. The Aztecs jumped into their canoes and paddled off home.

All of them felt content, for what they had seen at the temple had banished their worst fears. Huitzilopochtli, the Aztecs believed, died at sunset every day. As long as he received sufficient human sacrifices, he would come alive again at dawn. The afternoon's sacrifices had been plentiful. So now it was certain that tomorrow, the sun would rise over the white stone palaces and temples of Tenochtitlan. The crops, fruit trees and vegetables would continue to sprout. Life would continue as before.

And tomorrow, more human sacrifices would be made to ensure that every sunrise, Huitzilopochtli would come alive and the world as the Aztecs knew it would still be in existence.

What did it contain, this world which the Aztecs strove to prolong in such brutal fashion, by offering human sacrifices to their god? The most surprising thing about it was that it contained so many strange contrasts. In some ways, the Aztecs were remarkably advanced for their time. In other ways, they were remarkably backward.

In 1519, when the Spanish *conquistador* (conqueror) Hernán Cortés first penetrated into Mexico, he and his army were astounded at the size and splendour of Tenochtitlan. The Aztec capital with its 350,000 inhabitants and 60,000 houses was far larger than any European city of the time. Three huge causeways, two or three miles long (3-5 km) and each wide enough to allow ten horsemen to ride side by side along them, linked Tenochtitlan to the shores of Lake Texcoco. Double pipelines carried fresh water into the heart of the city. A dyke ten miles (16 km) long protected the Aztec capital against flooding.

The Aztec king, Moctezuma Xocoyotzin, lived in a huge palace. It contained one hundred rooms, one hundred steam-baths, twenty entrances and a main hall that could hold 3,000 people.

Artist's impression of Tenochtitlan

One Spaniard explored the palace till he was tired out, 'and never saw the whole of it.' What he did see was magnificent. The walls of the rooms were covered in marble, jasper and other rare materials. The ceilings were made of finely carved pine and cedar. The palace grounds contained irrigated gardens full of trees and tropical flowers, as well as aviaries and zoos stocked with exotic birds and animals.

Yet strangely, the people who had constructed so grand a city were primitive in many aspects of their lives. For instance, the Aztecs did not use the wheel for transport and had no animals to draw their ploughs. The only beast of burden they employed was Man himself. Long lines of porters would tramp through the mountain passes towards Tenochtitlan carrying on their backs the cotton, jade, feathers, gold, jewels, skins, agricultural produce and other goods that came into the capital from the outlying areas of the vast Aztec empire.

When the goods reached the markets of Tenochtitlan, they were bought and sold mostly by barter. This form of trade, where one commodity is exchanged for another, is normally used only by primitive peoples.

These were not the only curious contrasts that existed in the world of the Aztecs. To give another instance, Aztec knowledge of astronomy was far greater than European knowledge. Aztec astronomers, all of whom were priests, knew how to plot and chart the movements of the Sun, the Moon and the planets, and recorded their observations in the form of geometric and other mathematical symbols. European knowledge of astronomy did not begin to reach this standard until well into the 17th century.

And yet the Aztecs, who were so much in advance of Europeans in this very complex science, were living partly in the Stone Age, the way Europeans had lived before about 2000 BC.

In Stone Age Europe, flint, stone, wood and other non-metal substances were used to make weapons, household utensils, tools and other implements. More than three thousand years later, the Aztecs were still using them, whereas Europeans had long ago advanced to using metals. The Aztecs knew about metals, but used them only for decoration. With metals like gold, silver, copper and bronze, the Aztecs made jewellery or embellished buildings and idols of their gods.

At the New Fire ceremony shown here, the old altar fire was extinguished and a fresh one lighted in the open breast of a victim slain for this purpose

A priest foretells the sex of an unborn child

Perhaps the strangest contrast of all however in the part-advanced, part-backward world of the Aztecs was the way they regarded themselves and their destiny.

On the one hand, they were consumed with fear at their own human weakness. They felt helpless before the terrifying powers of Nature and the gods they worshipped. If Huitzilopochtli and the other gods were angry with them, the Aztecs believed the world would come to an end. This was why they made human sacrifices – to keep the gods happy. It also explained why the Aztecs were so superstitious. They refused to construct a building, go to war, get married or do anything else important until the priests had consulted the stars and pronounced the time to be favourable.

On the other hand, the Aztecs entertained very high and mighty ideas about the position they occupied in the world.

Huitzilopochtli, they believed, had promised that they would be a master race. Non-Aztecs would exist only to serve them and supply them with food, goods and victims for religious sacrifices.

Huitzilopochtli,
the god of war

By the start of the 16th century, when the Aztecs ruled over an empire of some twelve million people, 100,000 square miles (over 250,000 sq km) in extent, it was not difficult for them to think that the wonderful promises of Huitzilopochtli had come true.

The sign from Huitzilopochtli

Only two centuries before, the Aztecs had been poor nomads, wandering from place to place in search of a home. They had nothing but animal skins to wear, and often no place to sleep but mountain caves. They lived by hunting, or by hiring themselves out as soldiers to richer tribes. Sometimes they managed to stay in one place for a few years, by serving other tribes as vassals. But in the end, they were always thrown out and forced to move on.

If the Aztecs were treated as outcasts by other peoples in Mexico, there was a very good reason for it. They were horribly ferocious and had already begun to sacrifice humans to their gods.

Once the Aztecs fought a battle on behalf of the Lord of Calhuacan, and afterwards brought him a bag containing the ears of 8,000 prisoners. It was a truly grisly way to show how many men they had captured. No wonder other, milder-natured Mexicans were shocked by the Aztecs.

At last the Aztecs arrived at Lake Texcoco, and found a place where they could settle down. It was not a very pleasant place. There was nothing there but marshy swamp and uninhabited islands swarming with mosquitoes. Nevertheless, according to Aztec tradition, Huitzilopochtli himself had decreed that this uninviting site would be their home. One day in 1325, an Aztec priest saw an eagle perched on a prickly-pear cactus. This the priest claimed was a sign from Huitzilopochtli. So here the Aztecs built a temple, and round it a collection of reed huts. They began to eke out a miserable existence by fishing for food in the lake, hunting for waterfowl in the marshes and doing a little trade with neighbouring tribes.

It was a hard struggle for the Aztecs to survive in such terrible conditions. Yet within a few years, the cluster of huts in the swamps of Lake Texcoco began to grow into the city of Tenochtitlan (the name means, 'the place of the prickly-pear cactus'). Not long afterwards, the Aztecs set about conquering the tribes around them. At this, they were very successful. By 1440, the Aztecs had overrun the entire Valley of Mexico.

The Aztecs gather tribute from their subjects

Within another eighty years, they had overcome the Tepanecs, Tarascans, Mixtecs, Totonacs and other tribes to rule a vast empire which stretched from the Gulf of Mexico to the shores of the Pacific Ocean. (See map at front of book.)

Within this huge area, there were thirty eight provinces, inhabited by subject peoples who were little more than serfs to their Aztec masters. The Aztecs' subjects had to send the best of the crops they grew, the pick of the manufactures they produced and any luxuries they had as tribute to Tenochtitlan.

Of course, the Aztecs were heartily detested by the conquered tribes who were however helpless before the power and efficiency of their masters. The Aztecs' subjects could do nothing but pay up and pray that somehow, some day, they would get their revenge.

The payment of crops, goods and valuables was only part of the tribute the Aztecs demanded from their subjects. They also had to supply people to act as human sacrifices in the temples, and to serve the Aztecs as slaves. Men and women were forced to leave their homes, never to return, and make the dismal journey to Tenochtitlan in obedience to the Aztecs' wishes. No one knows how many there were but they must have been very numerous. The Aztec priests sacrificed between ten and fifty thousand people a year and thousands might be slaughtered at one time, on special occasions. In 1473, the *teocalli* or twin temple to Huitzilopochtli and Quetzalcoatl (bringer of civilisation) was inaugurated. Priests worked day and night for four days killing 20,000 victims. They stood in four lines stretching for two miles (3.2 km) through the streets of Tenochtitlan. It was a horrible fate, made all the more ghastly by the fact that the priests were terrifying to look at. They painted themselves black all over and wore cloaks decorated with skulls and bones. They never washed or combed their long black hair, but left it permanently matted with the blood of their victims.

Every so often, a slave who had misbehaved was among the slaughtered thousands. A lazy, rebellious or thieving slave could be returned to the local market to be sold again. There he would stand with a wooden yoke around his neck while prospective buyers looked him up and down. A bad slave was allowed to have only three successive owners. If all were dissatisfied with him, there was only one thing left: the slave was sold to the priests to be sacrificed in the temples.

Nevertheless, despite their cruel ways, the Aztecs acted justly towards slaves who behaved themselves. No good hardworking slave could be sold by his master unless he agreed to it. Any slave had the chance of buying his liberty by repaying his owner the price originally paid for him.

Stairway to the temple of Quetzalcoatl

A slave tries to escape

Because the children of slaves did not automatically become slaves in their turn, it was possible for Itzcoatl, the son of a slave-girl, to be elected king of the Aztecs. After his election in 1427, Itzcoatl masterminded the spread of Aztec power throughout the Valley of Mexico and was one of the greatest Aztec kings.

This was a destiny his mother could not have foreseen the day a slave merchant dressed her up in borrowed clothes to make her look attractive, and put her up for sale in the market. After she was sold, Itzcoatl's mother was put into a wooden cage, and there she waited until her owner came to collect her.

At her owner's home, she worked in the kitchens or spun thread, wove cloth and sewed cloaks and other garments. Male slaves worked in the houses as servants or carriers, or they toiled in the fields, growing maize, chillis, tomatoes, squash-fruit and other crops.

While they remained slaves, these people occupied the lowest and most humble place in Aztec society. Just above them, but not much better off, were the *mayeques*. Mayeques were officially free men and women, but in order to live, they were usually forced to give themselves up into a kind of bondage. They rented land from Aztec nobles or priests and paid for it by giving up most of the crops they grew upon it. A mayeque's life was miserable indeed, because after he had paid his dues to his landlord, he was usually left with barely enough to live on.

Some mayeques had known better days as free commoners and members of the twenty hereditary clans into which the Aztec nation was divided. A free commoner became a mayeque because he had got into debt or committed some crime. It was a dreadful disgrace, for it meant that the commoner and his family ceased to be members of their clan. With that, they lost their right to farm their share of the lands owned by the clan.

Whether they were mayeques or commoners, all Aztec farmers had hard lives and did much back-breaking work. They had no animals to draw ploughs and dig furrows in which seeds were planted. So planting had to be done the hard way, by hand. Aztec farmers used a digging stick to punch holes in the ground and dig out a small amount of earth. Then they dropped seeds into the holes and covered them up by smoothing the earth with their bare feet.

Maize

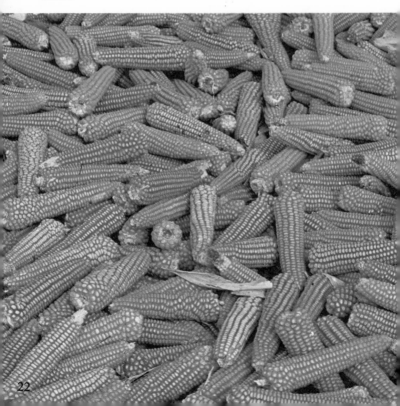

Baking tortillas

The crop which Aztec farmers planted more than any other was maize, which they ate in many different forms. There were baked maize cakes called *tortillas* and *atole*, a maize porridge seasoned with pimento or sweetened with honey. *Tamales* were a sort of pie filled with mushrooms, pimento, beans, fruit, frogs, snails or lizards.

As for meat, the farmers reared turkeys and edible hairless dogs, while country dwellers were able to hunt for *peccary* (a type of pig), deer, rabbits, hares and coyotes.

The most fortunate farmers were those who grew crops on the *chinampas*, the so-called 'floating gardens' that were permanently moored in the waters of Lake Texcoco. These artificial islands were made by heaping up a tangled mass of water plants and covering them with mud from the bottom of the lake. The mud was extremely fertile, and the farmers could grow almost anything on it – maize, flowers, chillis, tomatoes, and squash-fruits.

The large chinampas could be about 300 ft (92 m) long and up to 30 ft (10 m) wide, and some Aztec

Present-day floating garden

farmers built their homes on them. They were made from cane and reeds. It was quite safe to live on a chinampa, because they were anchored to the lake bed by the roots of willow trees which were specially planted for this purpose.

Out in the countryside, Aztec farmers lived in one-room huts made of earth or stone, with thatched roofs. Every hut had its own small shrine, containing images of the gods made from wood, clay or stone. Each had its stone hearth where the cooking was done on a fire of burning leaves, bits of wood and dried cactus.

Four out of every ten Aztecs were free commoners belonging to the clans, and it was their taxes that supported the government, the army, the priests and the king and his court. They also paid for the rulers of the clans, their local schools and the welfare services that supported less well-off people like widows, orphans, the old and the sick.

The commoners did not pay their taxes in money but in goods, like food or lengths of cloth. From time to time, people 'paid' taxes by constructing or repairing buildings, or by collecting wood for the temple fires.

The ruling class of Aztecs, the *tecuhtli*, were not expected to pay taxes. From their ranks were drawn army generals, government officials, judges in the law courts and the nobles who served the Aztec kings. As befitted their high positions, the tecuhtli were given fine houses to live in and the lands that went with the office they occupied. A tecuhtli was treated with great courtesy and respect and people would add the ending '-tzin' to his name every time they spoke it: '-tzin' meant something like 'Sir' or 'Your Grace'.

If your father was a tecuhtli, you automatically belonged to the aristocratic class called *pilli*. Because these young nobles were the future leaders of the Aztec nation, they were given the best education the Aztecs could devise.

Education for an Aztec meant only one thing: he or she was to be trained for the role in life decreed by Aztec custom and tradition.

Aztec boys were destined to become soldiers.

A tecuhtli family at home

They would fight the enemies of the Aztec nation, and supply the priests with enough prisoners to act as sacrifices to the gods. In addition, boys were supposed to follow in the footsteps of their fathers. The boys were 'informed' of these facts during their naming ceremonies. After a baby had been washed and laid on a cradle of rushes, the midwife sprinkled water over him and recited prayers to keep him free from evil and misfortune. Then, the baby was presented with tiny versions of a shield and arrows, the tools of the soldier. He was also given the symbols of his father's profession. If the father was a farmer, these would include a digging-stick and the seed-bag farmers hung around their necks at planting time.

Naming an Aztec child

A craftsman's son working on a mosaic head

If his father was a craftsman, then the boy would receive any of several types of tools. They might be implements for making feather costumes, head-dresses, capes, fans, armbands or pictures. They could be the tools metalworkers used to produce copper needles, fish hooks and small axes, or gold and silver jewellery, nose-rings or lip-plugs. Other Aztec craftsmen worked in jade, turquoise, rock crystal, amethyst and other precious stones. Or they were potters, tailors, stonemasons or carpenters. But whatever the fathers did for a living, the general rule was that their sons were going to do the same.

As for the girls, they were to be wives, mothers and homemakers. So, when they were named, girls were presented with miniature symbols of the housewife – a tiny spindle, a work basket and a broom.

Five years after the daughters were named, mothers started to train them for their allotted role in life. The girls were shown how to weave thread, grind maize, cook meals and look after babies. Meanwhile, Aztec boys were following their fathers round the fields or the workshops. There they would learn the skills they would need to do their fathers' jobs.

Most Aztecs accepted these rules of life without question because they were brought up to be totally obedient to authority. From their earliest childhood, they were taught to obey the king, the priests, the law, the elders of their clan, their parents and above all, Huitzilopochtli and the other Aztec gods. They even had to obey commands that they die on the altars of the gods if that was expected of them. Many did so willingly and even gladly. They believed their blood was needed to nourish the gods, so the gods must have it. In any case, the Aztecs thought death in war or on the sacrificial altar was a marvellous destiny. By this means, they would be instantly transported to the Sun-paradise of Huitzilopochtli.

How did the Aztecs become as obedient as this? The answer was very harsh discipline for those who misbehaved. Rebellious or lazy children were flogged, or held over a fire made of chilli peppers and forced to breathe in clouds of bitter-smelling smoke. Either that or they had cactus spines driven into their flesh: afterwards, their hands and feet were tied together and they were forced to lie on wet soggy ground for a whole day.

This discipline was imposed both in the home and at school.

An Aztec girl being trained

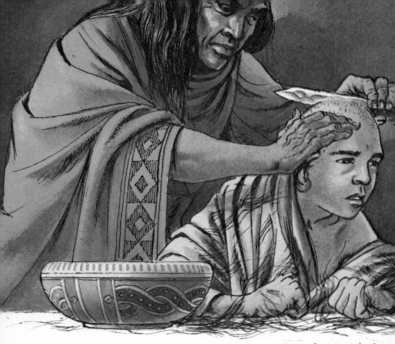

A pupil is punished

There were two kinds of schools for Aztecs. At one, for the children of commoners, boys were taught by soldiers how to fight in battle and how to observe religious rituals. To toughen them up, pupils were forced to sleep in cold, draughty rooms with only a light covering. Laziness or misbehaviour was punished by burning off a pupil's hair and shaving his head.

At the *calmecac* schools where the children of the tecuhtli were educated, life was even more uncomfortable. The boys had to do humble work, like cleaning and sweeping or digging the land. On certain days they were not allowed to eat.

On certain nights, they had to climb into the mountains where shrill winds whined among the rocks and every shadow might turn out to be a demon of darkness. While the night passed, the boys had to drive cactus spines into their ears and legs until they bled. At other times, boys had to get up at midnight and plunge into pools of ice-cold water. All this was intended to make calmecac boys able to conquer fear and ignore pain and discomfort.

At a calmecac school for girls, pupils used to get out of bed several times a night to say prayers and burn incense to the gods. Talking at meals and at other times during the day was forbidden. If a girl spoke to a boy at any time, she was severely punished. And if she stopped work without permission, even for a moment, she could be flogged.

A calmecac boy alone at night on a mountainside

Perhaps it was just as well that the children of the tecuhtli were so harshly treated for breaking rules at the calmecac schools. Later, in adult life, these nobles were expected to set an example to the mass of Aztec commoners. This was why they were treated with extra severity if they broke the law.

The son of a commoner who stole from his father was sold into slavery as a punishment. A nobleman who committed the same crime was put to death. For being drunk, the commoner was sentenced to have his head shaved and his house demolished. Only if he was convicted of being drunk a second time was a commoner

executed. Nobles were given no second chance: the first time they were found guilty of drunkenness, the High Court sentenced them to death.

The High Court sat from daybreak to sundown at the royal palace in Tenochtitlan. It was presided over by the Ciuacoatl, the man who was second in rank only to the king. The Ciuacoatl and his assistant judges used to give judgement in all cases concerning nobles or high officials. They also heard more complicated cases, like disputes over field boundaries. Commoners were tried in small local courts, or if their crimes were very serious, in a higher court.

A case is tried

The Aztecs had odd ideas about what a serious crime was. They were very concerned that everyone in society should 'know their place'. So they made it a crime punishable by death for people to wear clothes belonging to others of a higher or different rank.

The wearing of sandals was one example. Only two people were allowed to wear sandals within the royal palace: one was the king, the other was his Prime Minister. Everyone else had to walk barefoot. If they failed to do so, they were executed. Within the city of Tenochtitlan, only noblemen could wear fine painted sandals covered in gold leaf. Soldiers who had performed great deeds in battle could also wear sandals, but they had to be cheap and roughly made. Everyone else had to walk the city streets in bare feet.

The laws of the Aztec state were, of course, very harshly enforced.

Everyone had to obey them or suffer punishment. However, there was one group of Aztecs who lived outside the state laws, like a state within a state. These were the merchants who each year journeyed through

Goods ready for packing

and beyond the Aztec lands on long trading missions. The merchants had their own god, Yacatecuhtli (lord who guides), and ran their own courts of law. They had their own guilds, which were like trades unions, and lived in their own district in Tenochtitlan. Nobody could become a merchant or join a guild unless his father was a merchant. It was like an exclusive club.

When the time came to plan a trading mission, various merchants joined forces and gathered together a great stock of goods. There were gold ornaments, pieces of pottery and other items made by craftsmen.

There were herbs, needles, furs, clothes, capes, spices, rope, medicines, feathers, and quantities of salt, obsidian (black volcanic glass) and other raw materials. These goods were carefully packed ready to be loaded onto the backs of the porters who would make up the trading 'caravan'.

The night before a trading mission set out was a solemn time for the merchants and their families. Everyone knew the great dangers a trading caravan faced. The merchants would have to cross deserts, perilous mountain passes and fast-flowing rivers. They might be attacked by hostile tribes or die from infected drinking water, bad food or exhaustion.

Of course, the stars had been consulted and the date fixed for the merchants' departure was known to be a 'lucky' one. But even so, leave-taking was a sad business. Years might pass before the merchants returned to their wives and children. To show they would be thinking of each other while they were away, the merchants and their families washed their heads and cut their hair. None of them would do these things again until the merchants were safely home.

Then the merchants slipped quietly away from their homes and set off on their journey. With them went a strong force of soldiers, to protect them against attack, and to bully foreign tribes who were unwilling to trade. In their high-handed way, the Aztecs looked on people who refused to trade as enemies and they were quite prepared to start a war in order to force foreigners to barter their goods.

A trading mission sets out

Naturally, the merchants were greatly feared and hated and not only because they were prepared to use violence in order to do business. Foreign tribes knew that Aztec merchants acted as spies for the government in Tenochtitlan. They would gather information about the wealth and military strength of the lands through which they travelled and then report their findings to the king. If the lands were worth the trouble and expense, the king would send an army to conquer them.

As many vanquished tribes discovered, the Aztecs were superb soldiers, and used weapons that could do terrible damage. One was the *maquihuitl*, a cross between a sword and a club. It had a shaft of hard wood about 3ft (92 cm) long set with pieces of razor-sharp obsidian. As the Spaniards found to their amazement, a maquihuitl could sever a horse's head from its neck. The

Aztecs also used javelins tipped with obsidian, which they flung by means of an *atlatl* (spear-thrower). Aztec arrows, which were usually about 5 ft (150 cm) long, also had obsidian tips.

Aztec soldiers protected themselves with a thick padded suit made from cotton soaked in salty water. It stretched from the neck to the knees. Their shields were usually round, and measured about 2.5 ft (77 cm) across.

One of the Aztecs' most effective weapons was their appearance and the noise they made before a battle began. They used to frighten their enemies by banging drums, or by blowing deep, baleful notes on conch shells or shrill screaming sounds on whistles.

Accompanied by these unnerving sounds, an Aztec army would sweep forward led by knights dressed in feathered head-dresses, and the skins of savage beasts like the jaguar. From high above the mass of Aztec soldiers, fierce faced images of eagles or ocelots (small leopards) glared down on the enemy from feathered banners. More than one opposing army, confronted by all this menace and power, panicked and ran away. Those who stayed to fight usually received a sound thrashing, because the Aztecs possessed the best army in the whole of Mexico.

At least, it WAS the best until 1519 when Hernán Cortés sailed for Mexico from the Spanish colony of Cuba with a fleet of 11 ships, 508 soldiers, 100 seamen, 16 horses and 14 cannon. The Spaniards were tough, enterprising adventurers.

The coast where the Spaniards landed

They had been drawn to Mexico by tempting tales of its gold, silver and precious jewels. They also wanted to add Mexico to the colonies Spain already possessed in the New World of America – in the Caribbean, Brazil and Panama. However, in the Aztec Empire, Mexico offered the greatest prize yet encountered by any colonising Spaniard and Cortés was determined to make himself master of it.

First, though, he would have to reach the heart of the Empire – Tenochtitlan. That, of course, meant a difficult, dangerous trek into mountains which were, in places, over 18,000 ft (5,486 m) high. In mid-August 1519, Cortés and 400 Spaniards set out across the steaming hot coastal plain. Soon they were climbing up into the mountains through thick tangled forest, and emerged onto the high mountain plateaux.

As the Spaniards struggled through the mountain passes, they were chilled to the bone by icy, piercing winds. It was difficult to breathe at this altitude and the Spaniards stumbled along, gasping and dizzy. From time to time, hostile tribesmen attacked them with boulders and stones and showers of poisoned arrows. Scores of Spaniards were killed. The survivors began to grumble and demand that Cortés turn back. But Cortés would not hear of giving up. At last, on 2nd November, the Spaniards marched through the pass between the twin volcanoes Popocatapetl and Ixtacihuatl, and down through more thick forest into the Valley of Mexico. Six days later, after a terrible eleven-week journey, Cortés led his men along one of the great stone causeways that led into Tenochtitlan.

The country the Spaniards marched through, with the volcano Popocatapetl in the background

An amazing sight greeted them. Aztecs were crammed in the streets and on rooftops and crowded into canoes on the lake and canals. The richer ones were decked out in brilliant feathered and bejewelled head-dresses and cloaks, and were adorned with gold and silver ornaments. Suddenly, Cortés saw a magnificent litter approaching. It was decorated with green feathers and gold and silver hangings. Inside sat King Moctezuma Xocoyotzin, dressed in sumptuous robes and wearing sandals encrusted with precious stones and soled with gold. The litter came to a halt. Moctezuma stepped out and walked towards Cortés across a carpet of cloaks being laid on the ground by servants. Four nobles held a canopy of green feathers over Moctezuma's head. They kept their eyes on the ground, for the Aztecs thought it a sin to look directly at the king.

A feathered head-dress which may have been worn by Moctezuma

Moctezuma and Cortés exchanged gifts of necklaces, and then the Spaniards proceeded into Tenochtitlan itself. There they were confronted by even more stunning sights. Huge coloured floats made of sweet-smelling flowers lay on the water. Nearby, Aztec nobles awaited to greet the Spaniards with garlands, collars of gold, beads and finely woven materials.

Then came the most astounding surprise of all. Moctezuma bowed to Cortés and said: 'Lord, you have arrived to take possession of your throne . . . its people lie beneath your hand and under your protection! . . . Welcome to your kingdom, lord!'

The Spaniards could hardly believe their ears. Moctezuma appeared to think they were gods and he was handing his empire over to them of his own free will.

Even their horses were regarded as heavenly creatures, for the Aztecs had prepared beds of flowers for them to sleep on.

Cortés immediately realised the mistake the Aztecs had made. He knew of the old Aztec prophecy that the white-skinned god Quetzalcoatl would return to Earth from the east and claim the Aztec Empire. The Spaniards had white skins, and they had come eastwards from Europe, across the Atlantic Ocean.

Cortés knew he had to be careful, though. Here he was with only a handful of men, surrounded by thousands of Aztecs, high up in the mountains of a strange country. If the Aztecs suddenly realised their mistake, they might turn on the Spaniards and slaughter them.

So Cortés protected himself against this risk by imprisoning Moctezuma soon after his arrival in Tenochtitlan. With Moctezuma his captive, Cortés could tell him what commands to give his subjects. They would obey unquestioningly, as they always obeyed their king. And so it turned out.

Cortés demanded that the Aztecs swear loyalty to King Charles of Spain. Moctezuma ordered his nobles to do so. They obeyed him. It all seemed so easy. Cortés congratulated himself on his amazing luck. He had never dreamed the conquest of Mexico would be so simple.

Then things started to go wrong. In May 1520, bad news reached Cortés. A force of 1,400 Spaniards had arrived in Mexico led by Cortés' old enemy, Panfilo de Narváez. Narváez had come with orders from the Spanish Governor of Cuba, who also hated Cortés, to seize the conquistador and stop him taking power in Mexico. Cortés was forced to leave Tenochtitlan to deal

The Spaniards smash an Aztec idol

with this new danger. He drove Narváez away without much trouble and by June 24th was back in Tenochtitlan. His absence however had proved disastrous. Without their leader to keep them in order, the Spaniards had demolished the Aztecs' idols, robbed their temples and forcibly converted them to Christianity. As a result, the Aztecs were in a murderous mood.

Soon after Cortés returned, they mounted a violent attack on the Spaniards, killed one third of them and drove the remainder out of Tenochtitlan. When Moctezuma tried to stop the fighting, he was showered with stones by the rebels and died soon afterwards.

Cortés was furious. The Aztec Empire had so nearly come within his grasp. Now he would have to fight for it. He planned his attack carefully.

First, he ordered ships to be built so that they could bombard Tenochtitlan from the lake with their guns. Next, he took advantage of the hatred the Aztecs inspired among their subjects and persuaded thousands of them to join him. The Mexicans were only too pleased to do so. At last, with the Spaniards' help, the Aztecs' long-suffering subjects were going to get their revenge.

By the end of 1520, everything was ready. On December 27th, Cortés set out once more for Tenochtitlan, leading an army of 540 foot-soldiers, 40 men on horseback and 100,000 Mexicans. The long and bloody siege of Tenochtitlan which followed destroyed most of that beautiful city and killed about 240,000 of its inhabitants. Cortés' men cut off the water and food supplies.

For days on end, his ships pounded away at the Aztec capital with salvo after salvo of cannon fire. As the Spaniards and their allies fought their way into Tenochtitlan, the Aztecs resisted ferociously. They deluged the attackers with arrows, stones and other missiles. Captured Spaniards were sacrificed to Huitzilopochtli. Day and night, the Aztecs prayed and sacrificed to their god, begging him to aid them. They prayed in vain. Cortés' army pushed deeper and deeper into the city, killing and destroying as they went. Soon the streets and canals were choked with the rubble of wrecked houses and temples and piles of dead bodies.

At last, on 13th August 1521, it was all over. That day, Tenochtitlan – or rather, its smoking, blood-stained ruins – finally fell into Spanish hands. With that, the Aztec Empire came to its end, and so did the world the Aztecs had known. For the Spaniards, whose own empire in Mexico lasted until 1821, tried to destroy every trace of Aztec civilisation. They pulled down the Aztec temples and idols and built churches over the ruins. They constructed a new capital, Mexico City, over the rubble of Tenochtitlan. They burned the sacred books of the Aztec priests and forced the Aztecs to become Christians. The Aztec hereditary clans were disbanded and the clan members became the serfs and slaves of their Spanish masters.

The Spaniards did all this because they regarded the Aztecs as wicked, bloodthirsty people. Unfortunately, in destroying their wickedness, the Spaniards also destroyed much of the splendour and achievements of Aztec civilisation.

The Cathedral in present-day Mexico City

Today, not much remains to remind us of the poor wandering tribe which built up one of the first great empires in America. At least, though, statues of the Aztec gods have survived and from their fierce expressions, you can still get an idea of the forcefulness and power of the Aztec religion. The carved stone calendar or 'Stone of the Sun' discovered on the site of Tenochtitlan reveals the Aztec genius for astronomy. And the green feathered head-dress 4 ft (122 cm) high, shown on page 46, displays something of the grandeur and colour the Spaniards saw when they came to Tenochtitlan as gods, and stayed to become conquerors.

INDEX

	Page
America	43, 51
Astronomy	10, 51
Atlantic Ocean	47
Atlatl (spear-thrower)	41
Atole (porridge)	23
Battles	15, 16, 17, 40-42, 49, 50
Brazil	43
Bronze	10
Calendar, Stone	51
Calhuacan, Lord of	15
Calmecac schools – *see* schooling	
Capes	39, 45
Caribbean	43
Cathedral	51
Causeways	8, 44
Ceremonies, Naming	28-29
Ceremony, New Fire	11
Chillis	24, 30
Chinampas (floating gardens)	24-25
Ciuacoatl (judge)	35
Clans	21, 27, 30, 50
Commoners	21, 22, 27, 32, 34, 35
Conquests	16, 17
Conquistador (Spanish conqueror)	8, 48
Cooking	23, 25, 30
Copper	10, 29
Cortés, Hernán	8, 42, 43, 44, 45, 46, 47, 48, 49, 50
Cotton	9, 41
Courts	34-35, 37

	Page
Crafts	29, 30-31, 37
Crime	36
Crops	17, 18, 21, 22, 23, 24
Cuba	42, 48
Discipline	30, 32, 33, 34
Education	27, 30, 31, 32, 33
Europe	8, 10
Farming	21, 22, 23, 24, 25
Feathers and featherwork	9, 29, 39, 42, 45, 46, 51
Flowers	24, 46, 47
Food	15, 21, 23, 24, 27
Gardens, Floating–*see Chinampas*	
Gods	5, 6, 7, 11, 12, 13, 14, 15, 18, 19, 25, 28, 30, 33, 37, 47, 50, 51
Gold	9, 10, 29, 37, 43, 45, 46
Head-dresses	29, 42, 45, 46, 51
Homes	24, 25, 26, 27
Huitzilopochtli (Sun god)	5, 6, 7, 12, 13, 14, 15, 18, 30, 50
Hunting	15, 23
Idols	10, 48, 49, 50
Itzcoatl, King	20, 21
Ixtacihuatl (volcano)	44
Jade	9, 29
Jewellery	9, 10, 29, 43, 45